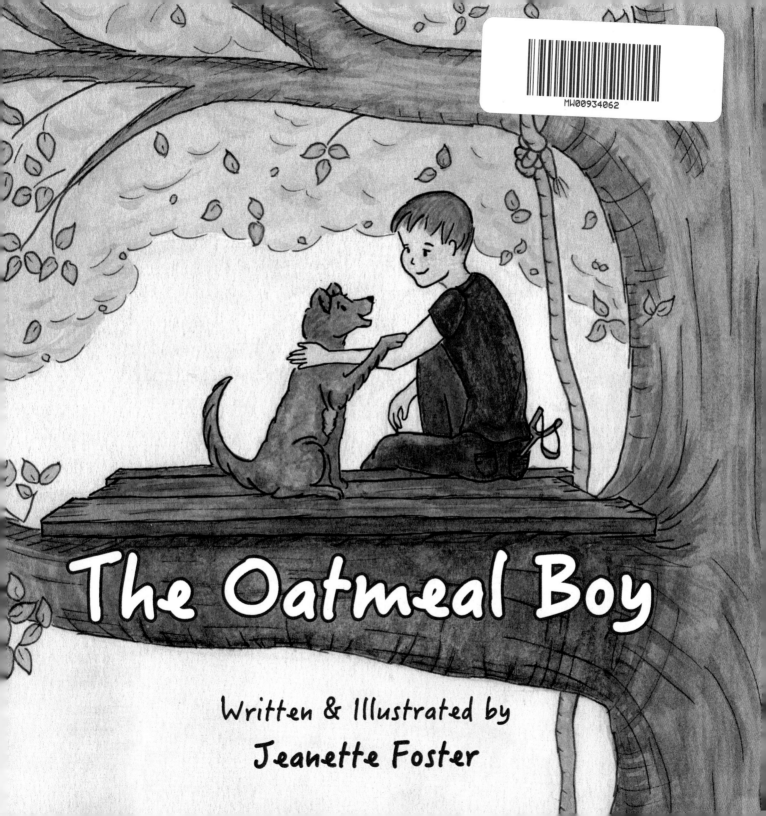

The Oatmeal Boy

Written & Illustrated by

Jeanette Foster

ISBN 978-0692742556

ArtsyJeanette@gmail.com

Dedication

This book would never have been possible apart from my Creator and Savior, Jesus Christ, who gave me the ability and inspiration, and my husband who constantly encourages me and makes all my dreams come true!

Emmit was a little boy
Just barely over ten.
He loved to play and climb the trees.
His pup was his best friend.

Emmit worked quite hard at play
So when the noon bell tolled,
He tumbled and ran to get back home
And into the kitchen he rolled!

Mother was the finest cook
The village ever saw.
She could bake bread and cakes and pies
Or biscuits without flaw!

It seemed the kitchen always knew
Of Mother's perfect touch;
A slice of any meal or mix
Was flavored oh so much!

Father was a handy man
Who could fix anything.
He traveled into town each day
And on his way he'd sing.

His father had a deep, rich voice
The village quite well knew.
He'd bellow out such lovely songs,
Grand hymns and old folk tunes.

Emmit's father loved his wife;
He called her "Dearie Mine,"
And all such sweet and sugar-ness
Made Emmit close his eyes!

"My Darlin', you make meals with love,
Your cookin' warms my heart,
But it's your eyes that make me smile,
I've loved them from the start."

"Oh, Oscar, you should shush such things,
Poor Emmit has covered his face!
But while he's not looking, sneak me a kiss,
Now here, give this porridge a taste."

She'd shove the spoon inside his mouth,
His eyes would light up with a smile.
His verdict was "Mmm!" with a kiss on her nose,
Then she'd stir it some more for awhile.

Emmit was glad his dad loved his mum,
But the kisses and hugs were all gushy!
It reminded him of the one meal he disdained;
It was lumpy and gritty and mushy!

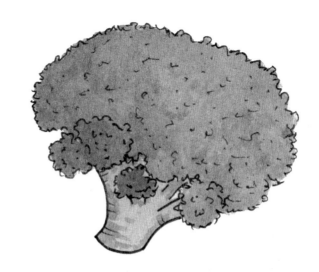

Yes, Emmit would eat anything his mum made,
The beets, and the greens, and the peas,
But when it came to eating THAT dish
He'd say, "No thank you please!"

He just couldn't stand it, he wouldn't succumb
To eating the bowl of warm meal.
Starving or not, he'd put down his spoon,
And away from the table he'd peel!

His mother did all that a mother could do
To make this small boy eat his food,
But no fixings or coaxings or proddings at all
Could convince him OATMEAL was good!

It all began when Emmit was small,
Just beginning to toddle about.
He once saw his grandad eating a bowl
And noticed his teeth...THEY FELL OUT!

So OATMEAL must certainly take out your teeth!
His grandpapa's smile said it plain!
From that day to this, he would resist
And not eat ONE bite - he'd refrain!

His mother would fix it all kinds of ways,
With sugar and raisins and cream,
Or honey and peaches and crunchy walnuts,
But still he would NOT his bowl clean!

So every morning for breakfast instead
He'd eat eggs or biscuits or toast.
His father would down his coffee and frown,
Then of Mother's OATMEAL would boast.

Poor Emmit would try to swallow a bite,
But the sticky warm oats wouldn't do.
He'd hang his head low, his tears wouldn't show
Then he'd whisper, "Can I be excused?"

One day after chores his father approached,
Asked if Emmit would make himself handy.
"I need two strong arms to come with me to town,
Besides, the job might bring some candy!"

His father smiled and gave him a wink,
Some CANDY! Of course he would come!
The general store was where they were going,
And where all the goodies were from!

So off they went down the mountain side,
They sang as they hiked the stone path.
Then before long, they entered the town,
The bustle of people they passed!

They entered the store with dust on their shoes,
Emmit went looking around.
The general store had goods of all kinds!
There was candy in mounds and mounds!

As he was looking at colorful twists,
Lolipops, gummies all sweet,
From the corner of his eye he spotted a girl!
She was watching him select his treat.

Her dress was soft blue, it brought out her eyes,
And freckles were splashed on her nose.
A ribbon to match in her braided, brown hair;
Emmit stopped looking and froze!

"Which one will you have?" asked her small voice,
"The cinnamon twists are the best!
They go good with tea, or honey toast too,
But with OATMEAL - better than all the rest!"

"OATMEAL! YUCK! Not THAT awful stuff!
No cinnamon stick will tempt me!
It takes out your teeth and makes you quite old!
I saw what it did to Grandpappy!"

"What are you talking about, silly boy!?
Oatmeal is perfectly good!
It turns little boys into great, big, strong men
And helps you to grow like you should!"

"Oh no, NO it doesn't! I've seen what it's done,
And besides, it tastes just like glue!
It takes out your teeth and wrinkles your skin!
I think it makes hair turn gray too!"

"Have you truly tried it?! I'm sure you're mistaken.
Oatmeal is like breakfast stew.
It goes well with nuts, and butters, and jams,
Alone it is heavenly too!"

As she defended her oatmeal mush
Her face looked quite convinced and sure.
She had both her hands placed on her hips,
Her feet planted solid and firm.

Emmit thought about what she had said;
He wasn't so sure she was right,
But then as he pondered she suddenly asked,
"Why don't you just try a bite!?"

There she stood with those bright, big, blue eyes,
To her kind smile how could he say "NO?"
He held in his breath and finally said "YES!"
Then sighed a long sigh deep and slow.

She ran to the back to get him a spoon,
Then scooped him his dish with delight.
On top of the mound, a sweet twist he found,
He no longer this battle could fight.

He squeezed his eyes shut, then dipped in his spoon,
His head felt the warm sweetness swirl!
His mouth was quite teased, his tastebuds were pleased!
The cinnamon twist made it whirl!

Spoon after spoon he shoveled inside,
And when the bowl's sides were scraped clean,
He wiped off his chin with the sleeve of his shirt,
Then sat back just smiling with glee.

"I knew you would love it!" the little girl laughed.
Her hands clapped together with joy!
Emmit gladly declared, "My teeth are still there!"
Then he shouted, "I'm an OATMEAL BOY!"

"What's this I hear!?" His father came in,
"Did you say you love oatmeal, my son!?"
"Yes, Father, yes! I loved every bite!
Her cinnamon twist made it fun!"

"Well done, good lad! Let's go tell your mum!
With pleasure her sweet smile will burst,
But seeing this bowl so empty and clean...
We better buy some more oatmeal first!"

THE END

Made in the USA
Monee, IL
10 January 2022

88252134R00026